I0648888

Paul Elmer More

Helena

And Occasional Poems

Paul Elmer More

Helena
And Occasional Poems

ISBN/EAN: 9783744770361

Printed in Europe, USA, Canada, Australia, Japan

Cover: Foto ©Andreas Hilbeck / pixelio.de

More available books at **www.hansebooks.com**

HELENA

AND

OCCASIONAL POEMS

BY

PAUL ELMER MORE

———

G. P. PUTNAM'S SONS

NEW YORK   LONDON
27 WEST TWENTY-THIRD ST.   27 KING WILLIAM ST,, STRAND

The Knickerbocker Press

1890

CONTENTS.

PART I.—HELENA.

PART II.—OCCASIONAL POEMS.

PART I.

HELENA.

" Adeste, hendecasyllabi, quot estis."

HELENA.

SNOW-WHITE Helena, for the noon was thirsty,
    Climbed with me to the fountain down the hill-side.
Silly Helena tossed her head to vex me,
Scorned the hand that I offered to assist her ;
Soon, however, ah me to say it, slipping
Down she fell in the mire.   Eheu the pity !
All the dryads above us in the tree-tops,
Laughed outright to behold her how she floundered.
Me she scolded, poor me, and but for scolding
Scarce would speak to me all that day, while moody
She lay stretched in the sun adrying.   Truly
I repented her sins ! but in the evening
As I kneeling before her scraped the clay off,
She stooped, meeker than is her wont, and kissed me,
Kissed me twice on the forehead in forgiveness.

II.

Bind me, bind me a wreath of white syringa
Fragrant-breathing ; and from their dewy covert
Tear me violets purple, tender-laughing ;
Also gather me roses dear to lovers,
Early roses with pungent yellow petals ;
Bind them all in a wreath to crown my Helen.
There the odors will mingle with the sweetness
Of her breath and her hair ; and there the petals
Fading, falling about her cheeks full-ripened,
Fading, falling, will tell how brief is beauty.

III.

Helen sat in the hallway where the breezes
Crowding in. through the door might fan her roses ;
There she sat with her needle darning stockings.
Helen smiled when I came and close beside her
Sat me down on a stool. Awhile I watched her,
Then in sport said I also darned quite neatly.
Straight she offered me thread and needle, bade me
Help her mend ; and I sat there sad and awkward
While she laughed me to scorn and called me booby.

IV.

All the lilacs were purple 'neath the window,
All the air was of gold when Helen bade me
Leave my papers and help her gather flowers :
You are taller, she said, and you can reach them.
Gladly went I, and never sight was fairer
Than my Helena 'mid the purple clusters.
See, she murmured, a nest among the branches,
Hidden there in the tangle.   And I told her
Soon the owners would come with merry music
Learned in sunnier climes, the pair of catbirds
Newly mated the year before who built it.
Favored shrub ! when thy odors all forsake thee,
What sweet melodies through thy leaves will tremble !

HELENA.

V.

Helen waded the shallow river with me ;
In my pockets I held her shoes and stockings,
While she tilted her gown and waded with me.
Here she leaned on my shoulder, for the pebbles
Bruised her sadly ; and yonder, almost falling
From that log in the middle which the mosses
Make so slippery, was she quite contented
While I held her ; and there where foams the current,
Almost screamed she aloud to feel the water
Rising over her ankles, splashing colder
Than ice.   Scarcely I knew myself for watching
How her toes in the water gleamed like pebbles.
Oh, were I but a fish to nibble at them !

HELENA.

Eheu ! Helena would not kiss me parting,
Would not, though in despair I pleaded with her.
There she stood with her hands behind her, mocking
All my arguments, though the milder night-wind
Sighed, I doubt not, and sighed again to hear me :
Stood there leaning against the door-post, smiling
At me down on the steps ; while still I lingered,
Hoping slily to slip my arm about her,
Hand to hand to oppose her stubborn courage.
Chide not, Mallon, she said, but leave me ; truly
Next time double I 'll give you.—Now I waver
Sadly buffeted 'twixt enjoyment hoped for
And vexation of disappointment.   Scarcely
Know I whether to call me sad or happy.

VII.

Helen's monitor tells me when my Helen
Startled feels in her breast the leap of passion.
For when love unexpected storms her bosom,
Rises ever within her throat, more rounded,
Softer, whiter than that of other virgins—
Rises ever a lump that doth bewray her.
There one day in my zeal I kissed her, found it
Sweeter fruit to the taste than Eden's apple.

VIII.

Helen lying dissolved in vesper slumber,
Once I found her, my Helen ; on her forearm
Drooped her face like a lily ; from her parted
Lips the breath of her heart came sweet as zephyr
Blowing over the rose.   Awhile uncertain
Stood I doubting within me, till in wonder
Bending over her, from her neck I lightly
Raised the mesh of her hair, and stooping kissed her,
Kissed her softly upon the throat.   She quivered
Turning slightly and murmured : Mallon, Mallon.
I stood looking upon her till her beauty
Filled my heart with amazement, till unconscious
From the chamber I stole and left her sleeping.

IX.

One day Helen and he who loves her, sitting
Where the shadows were cool upon the grasses,
In their idleness gathered leaves and wove them,
Leaves of oak and of maple, into garlands.
Helen, kneeling above him, on his forehead
Placed her wreath and declared him prince of poets,
Skilled to sing of the fairest maidens.   Mallon,
Where the daintiest ringlets all unconscious
Grew like buds in a snowdrift, set his garland,
Called her queen of the maids whose love inspired him.
Ah me, there in the shade they fell to kissing—
Now the poet must sing of joys remembered.

X.

Let the world, O my sweeting, scold for envy ;
While we love and are happy need we hear it ?
O my sweeting, to-night I prithee love me,
Kiss me, kiss me again : behold the shadows
Silent creeping recall that night of shadows
Which no dawn will disperse.   Ah, who will tell us
Whether loving I then will know you love me ?
Kiss me, kiss me again ; and on the morrow
All the gods I will pray that they may give you
Days in number as many as your kisses.

XI.

Eheu Helen, you dare to ask me pouting
Why so long I have shunned my dearest Helen.
Me you chide, on our night who came and waited,
Waited only to hear your maid, the ogress,
Smile and say : She is not at home, your Helen.
Falsest ogress ! beneath the curtain peeping
There I saw you with him I thought you hated.
All that night as I wandered through the city,
Here and there with the shadows, sad and anxious,
Mocked the stars from the sky and laughed, Behold him !

XII.

Autumn, fairest of all the seasons, autumn
Is come.   Blue is the air, a fainter cloud-land,
Scented too with the smoke of burning corn-stalks :
On the hill-side the gathered leaves and herbage
Blazing cover the sky with fragrant incense.
Oh, the woods and the streams and meadows ! truly
Autumn rules with a golden rod.   Now zephyr
Puffing over the hills, in slow succession
Stirs one tree then another, till the forest
Trembles all to the joy of perfect autumn.

XIII.

Low on Helena's neck toward the shoulder,
Lurks the daintiest mole among the lilies ;
Feeding there on the sweetest roots, no wonder
Softer, sleeker he is than other creatures.
When I watch him the lilies turn to roses,
Till he timid is hidden by their color ;
Never once have I touched him.   Foolish Helen,
I say, only a scar it is that lingers
Where one day when you met me, Amor shot you ;
Doubtless aimed at the heart but shot above it.
Eheu ! never the arrow, howe'er pointed,
Could have pierced to your heart within its fortress.

XIV.

Helen asked me in mischief why I loved her ;
Naught I answered but pointed to her mirror ;
Helen pouted and said 't was ill to tease her ;
Yet a week has elapsed since Helen scolded.

XV.

Yonder hollow o'ershadowed by that linden
Hold I sacred to Amor ; see his emblem
Carven deep in the bark : *To Love Triumphant.*
There one matin when scarce the dews were melted,
I found Helena like a lily languid
In its emerald bed, and crept beside her,
Laid my head in her lap, and bade her read me
What sweet legend had won her lips to smiling.
So outstretched in the grass I lay and listened,
While her hand on my forehead lightly rested,
Left it only to turn the page or wander
Idly over my features ; while her breathing
With its regular swell and cadence lulled me,
Till I dreamily wondered as I listened
How and where in her bosom lodged such music.

2

XVI.

Tears are dropping from all the trees and house-tops ;
Through the branches the wind goes sighing, sighing,
Heu, heu, Helena !—People say 't is raining.

XVII.

Helen threw me a kiss, and lo ! around me
All the air was suffused with balmy odor ;
Nay I doubt not if night had been that moment,
Thrilled with joy it had trembled into daylight.

XVIII.

Helen standing before the open window,
Half concealed by the woodbine round it climbing,
Smiled in mockery on me there below her.
Come down, Helen, I cried ; come down and kiss me ;
All the night I have waited for the morning.
But she laughed in her merry way to tease me,
Only tossed me a rosebud from her girdle.
Come down, Helen, I cried ; come down and kiss me ;
Sweeter sure is your mouth than any flower.
Just a moment she leaned from out the window,
Laughed, and murmuring said between her laughter :
Come up, Mallon, I prithee come and woo me ;
Many kisses have new-blown in the night hours.
Just a moment she leaned far out the casement
O'er me there in the garden, then she vanished.
So I turned to the door and rang and waited,
Rang and waited in vain, for no one answered
Save the sound of the distant bell faint-jangling.
Eheu ! only a rose I kissed that morning.

XIX.

All the world is aware and on the corners
Gossips, Helena now has young Narcissus.
Dismal Rumor who flying in the night-time
With her myriad eyes beholdeth all things,
Found me too unaware and poured her poison
Through my ears to the brain ; and now I wander
All undone through the city, heeding nothing.
Ah, what god will restore me ? lest the maidens
Point me out on the streets and titter saying,
See him, Helen he thought was true, poor Mallon.

xx.

Sweet my Helena, fairer than a flower
Gleaming white with the dew of early morning ;
Fair my Helena, now when all the meadows,
So long parched by the suns of torrid August,
Laugh together, and all the trees are happy,
Green once more from the showers as in April ;
Behold, Helena, scarcely know I whether
The fresh beauty of autumn stirs my bosom,
Or the love of a maiden, lately sleeping,
Wakes and moves in my heart with power redoubled.
So, my cosset, I come in doubt to see you :
Guard the door lest another coming sooner
Thrust me out in the night ; for thus together,
We two, Helena, haply you may tell me
Whether nature has charmed me or a maiden.

XXI.

Helen, lying among the coreopses,
Hid so long I had almost ceased to hunt her ;
When a ripple of laughter told her covert.
Forsooth ! there I beheld her laughing at me,
Her face peering above the yellow flowers
Like the spirit of autumn 'mid her people,
Her eyes merry with mischief, while a dimple
Flitted roguish about her mouth.   Oh, stupid !
Swift I ran to her side, and frowning sternly
Chid her froward ; and when she rudely tittered,
Printed deep in her throat the marks of anger,
Pressed them deep with my teeth to end her laughter.

XXII.

On a knoll in the park the firs and pine trees
Form a circle where in the shady centre
Spring the grasses molested by no footstep.
There I lay with my Helen, while the autumn
Breathing softly as summer all about us,
Set the herbs and the scattered leaves a-dancing.
From the spruce and the fir tree sweetest odors
Dropt upon us, while overhead the white clouds
Drifted slowly like sheep upon the meadows.
Seeking nothing I pulled aside the grasses ;
And there sheltered beneath the tangled herbage
Fairest violets, blue as eyes of maidens,
Smiled to greet me.   That day I still remember,
Kind was Helena, kind and fair was nature.

XXIII.

Snow-white Helena, you will read my poems,
Half reclined in the lap of young Narcissus,
While he points to the lines, your right arm hanging
Ah me ! loosely around his neck, your bosom
On his shoulder anear his cheek.   O careless
Heart ! what pang will discolor then your roses,
When you read of the hours our love made happy,
Of the quarrels we ended, Oh how sweetly !
Haply then in his arms you 'll pity Mallon.

XXIV.

Sweeter odor nor field nor forest offers
Than the scent of the osage orange ripening
In October.   Forsooth the air is nectar,
And we twain the immortals on Olympus
Tingling all with the draft ; yet now within me
Rarer odors are wafted.   You remember
How one day in the spring-time careless rambling
Stood we here by this hedge, and listening wondered
How such music was made in every tree-top ;
For the thrush and the catbird love these hedges.
Surely now you remember, when you asked me
Why the birds in the spring-time chaunt so gayly,
Straight I kissed you upon the mouth, and whispered :
Silly Helena, tell me first within you
What sweet melody now is welling upward.

XXV.

Ah, Narcissus, a sweeter joy you give me,
Robbing me of delight I deemed the sweetest ;
For you fill me with pity when I see you
Quite enthralled by the bliss I counted dearest,—
Pity sweeter than pleasure. Oh, you simple !
Sleeping now in her tender arms you dream not
Of the waking, alas ! too certain.   Truly
I too drank of her poppy, I too sleeping
Dreamed the joy of the world was in her bosom ;
Yet what waking has found me !   Fair and fragrant
Like a flower she is, that in the sunshine
Spreads her petals alluring bees to woo her :
One by one they alight and suck her honey,
One by one they are gone, and still she blossoms ;
Yet the winter will come, when brown and withered
On the earth she will fall and lie unnoticed.
Snow-white Helena, hear me while the time is ;
Lest the winter come on you unexpected ;
Lest men pass you in scorn ; and through the long night,
All unmoved on its hinges, dark and silent,
Hang your door that is wont to creak so often ;
For no mortal will turn it seeking Helen,
Helen sitting alone and old and ugly.

PART II.

OCCASIONAL POEMS.

"Amor, che nella mente mi ragiona."

TO THE GOOD SHIP "LA CHAMPAGNE"

(Which sailed from Havre, December 15, 1888).

I.

I SAW the vessel leave her port
   And sail into the west ;
Now heaven behold yon gallant bark,
For she beareth a lady blest.

May peace attend her o'er the sea,
And weather good and fair ;
Nor rougher gale smite her amain
Than the breathing of my prayer.

I saw her sink into the waves—
So hope, I thought, departs—
Till only a line of smoke was left,
Like memory in our hearts.

Now heaven forfend that I repine
Or hide me from the day ;
Though yonder boat that swims the tide,
Bear many a hope away.

2.

I hear the rain fall in the night,
Downrushing heavily ;
And Jesu Maria help !   I say,
How it must rain at sea.

I hear the drops clash on the waves,
As on an instrument ;
And murmur of the moving ship
With that far music blent.

I hear the water wash her decks,
And the rain dance on the boards ;
And I wonder what of dream or thought
To my lady it affords.

3.

The sun is smiling upon the land,
And smileth no doubt on the sea ;
A thousand delights are in the air,
And each of them I see.

I see a gleam o'er the water sweep
And flash the horizon round ;
And the waves are a thousand merry feet
That dance to a merry sound.

And my boat and the sea are a picture fair,
Begirt by a jewelled frame ;
And if there were naught beyond its rim,
My thoughts they were still the same.

My lady is sitting there on the deck ;
And if the jocund day
Bring a light to her eye and a smile to her lip,
I too will smile and be gay.

4.

In my dream a storm blew out of the north
And smote the shuddering main ;
The wind beat on the frantic waves,
Till I almost felt their pain.

Dear Lord, I cried, as Thou art good,
Pity the ships that are tost ;
If a love like my love followeth each,
What love were left if they 're lost.

I awoke in my trouble then, and lo !
A light serene in the sky ;
'T was only my heart that was beaten and tost
By doubts, I know not why.

5.

The belated moon is rising clear,
And the waves leap up in delight ;
I am glad she is come with her silver lamp,
For now I can see the night.

She holds her lantern above the flood,
And a light streams over the sea ;
And I know not whither that path may lead,
But it pointeth away from me.

A ship is sailing adown that road,
And the moon is lighting her on ;
And Oh, for the many she 's lighted before
And will light when my boat is gone !

I see the dark hull glide along,
Like a cloud alone in the day ;
I see the shadow of her smoke
Athwart the silver way.

I see the sailor pace the deck,
And hear his cry *All is well !*
The sound comes faint across the waves,
And my heart responds *All is well !*

6.

·Ah, sleep, my lady, never fear,
Be glad as thou art fair ;
For God is awake with all his power,
And I with all my prayer.

Ah, sleep, my lady, never fear ;
The moon is on the sea ;
Her light is brooding over the waves,
As my spirit broods o'er thee.

7.

I follow my boat afar, afar,
I follow her day and night ;
Now wherefor yonder fog drops down
To steal her from my sight ?

I see her plunge into the mist,
And close my eyes in despair ;
And I pray in the darkness of my soul,
For the boat in the darkness there.

8.

Now praise to God and to his powers
That rule the wintry main ;
Our ship is safe in port at last,
The gallant craft *Champagne !*

And my lady stands upon the deck,
And stilleth eager joy ;
For home is near and joys of home
No partings can destroy.

O Mary in heaven, so I pray,
My Mary to thee is dear ;
And thou wilt grant her every peace,
And give her every cheer.

O Mary in heaven, my spirit fails,
Shall I not call on thee ?
My lady on earth by a cloud of joys
Is wrapt and hid from me.

A DREAM.

IN my sleep last night I trode the shore
  Of the mighty, mighty sea,
And looked out over the throbbing waves
Toward the land that holdeth thee.

My dream was lonely and so I said
I 'll count the billows all,
 How many there are between us two,
As they rise and break and fall.

I counted a thousand and a thousand more,
And a thousand still in sight ;
And then I awoke or else I fear
I had counted there all night.

SLEEPLESSNESS.

L AST night again I could not sleep
      For weary thought of thee ;
It seemed I almost heard the hours
Slip by me stealthily.

I watched the moon move in the sky
And settle in the west ;
I watched the stars, and dreamed that there
Dwelt peace and hope and rest.

And still one thought was in my soul—
My God ! I 'gan to fear
My heart was haunted and I saw
The spirit, pale and drear.

UNREST.

L AST night and yesternight before
 I slept but could not rest ;
All day the waves sobbed on the beach,
All night within my breast.

Last night and yesternight before
The same dream haunted me,
A maiden's face so indistinct
I strained my eyes to see.

And if to-morrow night again
The sobbing waves I hear,
And if the same dream haunts my sleep,
My heart will break, I fear.

FRAGMENT OF A SUMMER IDYL.

I.

HERE in my lady's heart I 'll build me straight
   A tiny lodge, where soon and late
I 'll come for quiet when the myriad folk
   And chatter of the world provoke
A weariness of mind.　I 'll build it here
   Beside this merry brook to cheer
Me with its prattle as it bubbles by.
   Here in the bending grass I 'll lie
And watch the minnows darting in and out
   Among the stones ; while round about
The idle shadows drift now here, now there,
   So idle and so free of care,
The leisure of the years steals in the breast
   And fills it with untroubled rest.

Here in my lady's heart I 'll build me straight
  A tiny lodge, where soon and late
I 'll hide me for a season of repose.
  Upon its walls the hardy rose
And honeysuckle and some creeping vine
  Shall clamber at their will, and twine
And droop around the windows. Ah ! the hours
  I 'll sit as happy as the flowers,
And idle as the shadows that I 'll see,
  And quiet as the quiet tree
That rises near the door, forever still,
  Unmoved as an eternal hill.—
Yes, in my lady's heart I 'll build me straight
  A tiny lodge ; and o'er the gate
I 'll set this legend : " Never pain or care
  Or teasing thought or wan despair
Or worldly hope shall enter through this door,
  Where quiet dwells forevermore."

II.

The drowsy piping of the robin tells
  The well-known hour.   Right soon the bells
Will fling their slow reverberations out
  Across the misty air.   No doubt
The robin hath, but each new day will bring
  Old joys with never weary thing ;
And so each morning, ere the sleepy sun
  Hath tinged the east, I hear first one
And then another take the merry lay
  And sound his summons to the day.
The same sweet notes I hear each matin o'er,
  And say the bells will soon strike four :
And so for near an hour the same notes keep
  Me half awake, and then I sleep.

Sweet are the pipe and bell ; how oft they seem
  The merest music of a dream,
That hovers o'er my bed and glides away,
  Forever lost i' the glare of day.
And ever in the midst I see thy form,
  As veiled around, yet soft and warm,
Go floating by ; and all the idle dreams
  Are made more lovely, as the beams
Of Cythna, glimmering through their misty shroud,
  Lend a pale splendor to the cloud.

III.

The spirit of the night must sure have known
　　We were upon the lake alone.
He laid his wand upon the winds and blew
　　The clouds away ; he bade the dew
Not fall, and laid a spell upon the trees
　　To chaunt their sweetest in the breeze.
Our boat glode like a shadow on the lake ;
　　And ever the slow oars did make
A kind of music cadenced as they dipt
　　And hushed, then gurgling rose and dript.
And still before us on the ripples paced
　　The wanton moon, and still we chased
It o'er the water.   When we slackened, so
　　It stood and eyed us like a doe ;
Then stole we forward, but it leaped away
　　To lure us farther with its play.

At last I wearied of its mockeries ;
  And moored our boat beneath the trees,
Where the knit shadows fell so long and blind,
  Seek as it might it should not find
Us for a while. And here, I said, our boat
  Can lie as silent and remote
As any bark within a dream. Ah me !
  The very night is fair to see,
The very stars above can fill the breast
  With beauty till it feel opprest ;
Yet is it wonderful to me how one
  Sweet simple maiden can have done
So mighty havoc in my heart, and brought
  So mighty capture to my thought !
It may have been an hour—I only know
  At last we left our nook to go
Across the open lake, and down the stream
  So hemmed by trees that never beam

Of moon or star dropt in to guide our way.
  And ever as our pathway lay
Around some sudden bend, the narrow track
  Seemed swallowed in the tangled black
Obscurities. I know not how you steered ;
  I know not if the shadows weird
Filled you with awe : I only held the oars,
  The while we moved as if some force,
I know not what, impelled us on : and still
  You uttered not a word, until
I ceased to think and moved on in a dream.
  And when at last a sudden gleam
Showed that our row was ended ; still the spell
  Was on me, and I scarce could tell
If joy or sorrow held me, scarce could say
  My farewell as I turned away.

IV.

Sweet lady, take these flowers I bring to-day,
  And read there what I would not say.
Earth's arguments I call them which declare
  That truth and faith are not so rare,
And blossoms born of virtues lovelier still
  Unceasingly our hearts may fill.
Thus winter on the world may come and go,
  Thus spring within us too may blow.
Earth beareth in her breast a fair ideal,
  Which in the prime God maketh real ;
And we beholding whisper to our heart,
  Let not thy own ideal depart.
What though a bitterness our present foil,
  Are we not worthier than the soil ?
So take the flowers I bring, and they will say
  What I denied the other day.

4

v.

I stood one day beside a little pool,
   And watched the shadows, soft and cool,
Fall like a picture on its tranquil face.
   No ripple marred its quiet grace ;
I saw the mirrored beauty of the tree,
   And still beneath could plainly see
The limpid water and the bed whereon
   The sands like many jewels shone.—
A friend passed by and in his idle mood
   Threw in a random stone.   The rude
Concussion shook the pool and marred its grace ;
   Rough wrinkles swept across its face ;
The jeweled bottom rose like common soil
   To stain its purity and spoil
My crystal dream.   And so I left it then
   To settle till I came again.

VI.

I found one afternoon a pure white flower,
  A microphylla rose, that shower
And balmy weather had allured to part
  The outer petals round its heart,
And bare its snowy bosom to the sun.
  And so it was I plucked this one
White rose, and carried it a mile or more
  To give my lady fair ; and swore
All this I did for her dear sake, to show
  How like this flower she seemed to blow,
Unfolding all her beauty to my love.

.

And then I placed it just above
Her own white bosom, looking at her still
   While looking at the rose ; until
The witchery of her mouth o'ercame my eyes,
   And coming near to steal that prize
I lost them both from sight.   Alas, a child
   Cannot be more untamed and wild
Than I, a man !   For shame, she cried, the flower
   You gave has fallen in a shower
Of broken petals—see them, foolish man !
   She frowned, and stooping down began
To pick them one by one.   And then, with still
   A frown, she said, Some day you will
Remember how I gave you these with this :
   And with the leaves she gave a kiss.

THE HAUNTED TOWER.

A MONARCH on his marble throne,
Aweary of the court's turmoil,
Called for the sweetest singer known
To soothe him after irksome toil.

She stood before the haughty throng,
A goddess formed in purest art,
Herself more lovely than the song
That bore her fragrance to his heart.

Musician fair, the monarch cried,
Thou shalt be queen of all our land,
Our sweetest singer, dearest bride,
A pearl to deck our regal hand.

I sing for love of song, she said,
   And scorn thy pomp and royalty ;
Thy marble heart is cold and dead
   As is the white throne under thee.

The monarch started in his ire,
   And cast his sceptre on the floor :
" And thou shalt sing to thy desire,
   And thou shalt sing forevermore ! "

Deep in a sombre wood apart
   He reared a stately Norman tower,
A tomb built like a marble heart—
   " My haughty lady's singing bower."

And there he locked my lady proud,
   Within her palace and her grave ;
Where never cry, or low or loud,
   Might summon gentle heart to save.

My lady wanders in her home
　From silent stair to desert hall;
She singeth still, and from the dome
　The notes return, sweet spirits all.

Peace to my lady, tender dreams
　To her who sleepeth on the stones—
A broken flower whose odor seems
　To linger near in murmurous tones.

And often in a lonely hour
　The aged monarch steals from sight,
And whispers to the moaning tower,
　" My lady's spirit sings to-night."

And from the crumbled battlement,
　And through the ivy-mantled door,
Thou yet mayst hear her sad lament—
　My lady sings forevermore.

AN ORIOLE'S NEST.

A N oriole's nest in the leafless boughs,
　　Swayed by the wintry storm—
And I only think of the bird that is flown,
And the clime that is blooming and warm.

And the winter will go, and the spring will come,
And the leaves will bud and unfold ;
But the bird perchance may never return,
That was frightened away by the cold.

O LIMPID POOL.

O LIMPID pool so clear !
  Deep in thy silent dream,
The beauties rare of earth and air
  Like faery visions gleam.

And would that in my soul,
  Such worlds of wonderment
Might mirrored be, and give to me
  Thy dream of pure content.

MADRIGAL.

O LOVE, the sun mounts up
  Behind the eastern hills,
And from his golden cup
Like red wine pours the day across the night.
O joy ! and O delight !
And all the feathered quire,
Drunk with the gladness, fills
The world with music breathing sweet desire.
O Love, the sun mounts up
Behind the eastern hills ;
And from his golden cup,
I drink the wine that fills
My heart with madness like an eager fire.
Open the window, Love,
Behold I climb above,
And in thy white arms smother this desire.

SONG.

IF I were where my heart is,
   I 'd find my dreams, I know ;
And find the fairest maiden,
Whom they found long ago.

If I were where my dreams are,
I 'd find my heart, I wis ;
And find the dearest maiden,
And greet her with a kiss.

REGRETS.

A CURTAIN raised a foot or less,
　　And at the window there,
A woman's face of gentleness,
And an infant's round and fair.

A mother with her child, I say,
And that is all to thee ;
Yet as the car rolls on its way,
My heart sinks heavily.

A GREETING.

I KISS the breeze as it hurries by,
　And whisper soft a warning :—
My Love sleeps on though the sun is high,
Take her *that* for a fond good-morning.

You may wanton in her gown, and bare
Her lily, lily bosom ;
And then to appease her stoutly swear,
You thought it only a blossom.

TWO ROSES.

I MET a lassie on the car,
  And she was mickle fair ;
A white rose lay upon her breast,
And a red rose in her hair.

I sat not very close, I wis,
And looked not very long ;
And yet my heart was smitten sore,
And my heart felt very wrong.

My gentle maiden, so I said,
Thy rose so white and fair
How gladly had I given thee,
And the red rose in thy hair.

The white rose, I had even said,
Is that to me thou art ;
And the red rose burning near thy face,
The burning in my heart.

I gave thee neither this nor that,
Sweet maiden, mickle fair !
And I give thee neither touch nor kiss,
Yet I long to, mickle sair !

KATHARINE'S TOWER,

FRANKFURT AM MAIN.

I N the old square tower of Katharine Church,
  Far aloft in the smokeless air,
A woman dwells in her eagle home,
  With an only daughter, young and fair.

Below them swings the brazen bell,
  Silent and grim till at the hour
The ponderous hammer stirs and strikes,
  And the prisoned tones burst from the tower.

A lonely life these watchers lead,
  Where even the breezes hurry by ;
For the din of the city is swept away,
  And seldom a visitor climbs so high.

But at night when the world is all asleep,
 Save the stars above and the lamps below ;
I wis the girl is sitting there,
 In a fairy realm we cannot know.

A lonely life ! yet it seems to me
 My heart could rest in quiet there,
With the world and its people far below—
 In the lonely tower with its warden fair.

And still in the night when the streets are hushed,
 And the solemn bell tolls out the hour,
My thoughts mount up the mouldering stairs
 To the wonderful maiden there in the tower.

And wherever I go for many a month,
 The sound of that bell will haunt my heart ;
And the dream of a life in that starry home
 With the wonderful maiden will never depart.

5

AFTER THE OPERA.

I SAW the flower upon thy breast,
  And spoke not of 't, I know not why ;
So may my love as lightly rest
Upon thy heart and sweetly die.

The edelweiss is fair I know,
Yet doubly fair were 't worn for me ;
The edelweiss blooms in the snow,
Ah may thy bosom kinder be.

ONE MAY-DAY.

ONE May-day as I walked abroad,
 I marveled at the works of God ;
For all were full of flattery,
And every flower did smile at me.

I laughed in answer, Ah I know
Why all you blossoms flatter so ;
It only means, pluck me, pluck me,
And carry us your love to see.

O untaught children ! if I knew
My love who is so fair were true,
I 'd pluck you all—all I could bear,
And bind a wreath for her sweet hair.

And then a sadness clouded me,
While still they smiled in flattery ;
And then I knew the world so broad
Smiled not for me but for its God.

IN THE NIGHT.

HUSH, hush ! the clouds are still,
    And the stars utter no cry ;
The trees are wrapped in silentness,
    And the winds forget to sigh.

    They stand in silent awe,
    For God is passing by ;
They stand and utter no complaint,
    And I, what grief have I ?

WITH SOME COUNTRY ROSES.

TAKE these roses, lady dearest,
   Hold them to thy sweeter face ;
There perchance when they are nearest,
They may find a fresher grace.

How their petals droop together,
Hiding thus their dingy stains,
Wrought by long inclement weather,
And by long incessant rains.

So the love my heart would render
Hides itself in drooping fears ;
For however pure and tender,
It is marred by many tears.

LETTERS.

I BURNT the letters that you wrote,
   And watched them in the fire
Grow black and red and white and dead,
Upon their funeral pyre.

I watched them glimmer on the coals,
And saw them fall away ;
And as they burned my sweet love turned
To ashes cold and gray.

THE BURIAL.

I SLEPT last night a troubled sleep,
　　Through all my dreams I heard the deep
Faint tolling of a distant bell,
That still pealed out a dismal knell.

And in my dreams I seemed to see
Strange folk in slow solemnity
Move ever by, with downcast eyes
And lips that seemed to utter sighs.

And then I cried, What may this be?
Alas, quoth one weird shape to me,
Another mortal's joy is dead,
We go to lay it in its bed!

TO A PHOTOGRAPH.

D EAR Mary, sitting with your portrait there,
   I see the beauty of our fortnight rise,
Like an enchanted mist before mine eyes
Veiling the world about.   O time so fair !
If but recalling of thy joy could bear
Its hope to fill my sorrow with surprise !
Then not in vain I 'd link each dumb surmise,
Or sit before a picture half in prayer.
   Yet in the sadder years that end our race,
When all the passions of a life are told,
This faded portrait of a girl's young face
May turn the dull complaint of growing old
To sweet recital of an earlier grace :
I too was happy and have loved,—behold !

.

IN MEMORY OF AN AUTUMN DAY.

(October 16, 1886.)

I.

THERE is a time ere winter comes amain,
   Like peaceful twilight's calm that holds awhile,
When many things seem leaguers to beguile
The hours of labor from us, with the strain
And waste of getting ; when the winds are fain
To cease their moil ; and, like a sleeper's smile,
A misty veil is spread o'er sharp defile
And rugged top to smooth each line of pain.
I know not what the cause may be, I care
Not to inquire : yet with each dropping leaf,
And with each hushing of the drowsy air,
And muffling of each sound, some worldly grief
Is borne away, some thought we would not bear,
And gentle dreams steal in with sweet relief.

II.

Here will I lie beneath this spreading tree
And woo the sweetness of the day :—the stream
Of clouds o'er yonder boughs, moves in a dream
That through the bars of wakefulness I see ;
The hidden brooklet murmuring stealthily,
Bears on its bosom mingled sounds that seem
As echoes borne from unknown lands ; the scream
Of solitary crows that heavily
Move o'er the trees, is but the farewell cry
Of darker thoughts that leave me here alone ;
The breeze that creepeth up the hill with sly
And wayward steps, whispers in trembling tone
Of hopes I dare not hope, of hopes so high
They flit like visions o'er me and are gone.

TO " LA JOCONDE."

I FIND in beauty something fairer dwells,
  And all the semblances that satisfy
Arc but the trappings and the outer shells
  Of the sweet virtue that in them doth lie.

And they, the ornament of our brave race,
  In whom this spirit hides of loveliness,
Sweet women, wear its mystery on their face,
  A smile unnamed that lures to look and guess.

I wonder, knowing not if consciously
  This higher grace is theirs that I discern ;
And wonder deepens, till I seem to see
  A type beyond me of the grace etern.

O lady benedight, whom Vinci's skill
Hath given thy woman's charm to haunt us still.

A VISION.

A VISION of the watches of the night :
The City of our God, set like a jewel
Upon the utmost verge—O kind and cruel !
Bitter and sweet ! how mingled by the Might
That made them for what end ?   Behold the sight
Of that fair City, and the stately rule
And measure of its golden streets, the cool
Sequestered fountains, and the river's flight.

Behold the towering sapphire walls, and round
A stream of music ever flowing sweet,
A rampart strong, invisible, of sound.
And still behold ! the hideous throng that beat
Against its unseen bulwark, to rebound
Like flies that swarm the window's glassy cheat.

REFLECTIONS.

RIGHT often as I gazed upon the sea
  And over all the billows far and wide,
Meseemed each passing wave but rose and died,
To murmur in the air some mystery
Learned in the solemn depths where such may be ;
And once when the broad wind rose from the tide
And with the gathered burden louder sighed,
Meseemed I caught their utterance thus to me :—
  Live in the heart of things where warnings sleep
That tears and laughter are not idle farce ;
Live, not ashamed for honest pain to weep,
Still conqueror through sorrow's many wars,
Glad in the universal joys that keep,
And worthy of the sunlight and the stars.

HIDDEN MUSIC.

A S one who carries with him through the day
     The memory of music heard before,
While snatches of the half-forgotten score
Start on his lips or through his fancy stray ;
I wander with the burden of my lay,
Singing at intervals, though hearing more,
The music flowing from such hidden store,
And song that ere I fashion dies away.
    Thus too the toil of men, their idle word,
And the unremitting murmur of the street ;
Or melody of leaf-embowered bird,
And rustle of the clover at our feet,
Recall the perfect strains I somewhere heard,
Whose theme in part my broken songs repeat.

www.ingramcontent.com/pod-product-compliance
Lightning Source LLC
Chambersburg PA
CBHW032356020726

47499CB00008B/2770